How to become PRIME MINISTER

(in 7 easy steps)

Nigel Hastilow

Published by
Halesowen Press
WR11 7SA

www.halesowenpress.co.uk

*The opposition occupies the benches in front of you,
but the enemy sits behind you.*

WINSTON CHURCHILL'S ADVICE TO A NEW MP

This book is written for, and dedicated to,
the Digby Jones.

STEP 1

Become a member of parliament

'I have no idea who to choose.'

'No, nor me.'

'The trouble is, if you announce who it is publicly, you're stuck with it. Once you've made your choice you're lumbered.'

'And if they don't win…'

'Precisely. Nobody wants to join a sinking ship. It goes down with all hands.'

'And we're so new to this whole business.'

'Speak for yourself. Some of us have been there, done that, got the T-shirt.'

'Only on the local council, though. It's not the same thing at all.'

'Maybe not but the bitterness and resentment lasts just as long, if not longer.'

'If Dave wins, we're doomed.'

'You think so? If you ask me, he's the future and I intend to climb on board the bandwagon before it's really started rolling.'

'No, Dave's a disaster. It's got to be Neil.'

'Or Samantha. The Party needs a woman.'

'Or Malik. The Party needs someone from a minority.'

'Or Arivinda. She's the real deal. She's from a minority of a minority.'

'The country is still not ready for its first transgender ex-Royal Marine Prime Minister no matter how able she is.'

What are they on about? And who are they, anyway?

They are five new Members of Parliament, all elected to the House of Commons for the same political party on the same day at the same General Election.

They are discussing what is more or less the first decision they have to make – and it will be a decision which could have a dramatic, long-term effect on their political careers.

They have to vote for a new leader of their party. That's because the leader who was in charge for the General Election, the leader who until a few days ago was the Prime Minister of Great Britain and Northern Ireland, lost the election. He was now Leader of the Opposition and this defeat was too much for him. As soon as the result of the election was announced by the BBC, he said he would quit as party leader as soon as a successor was elected.

Everyone was glad to see the back of him. He'd been a pretty useless PM and led his party to a crashing defeat. Nobody liked him. From now on, he could go away and earn lots of money as an "international statesman". What that really means is he will become a paid speaker at conferences organised by groups like the National Federation of Caravan nd Holiday Home Manufacturers or the Jordanian Entrepreneurs Club (including free first class tickets to Jordan and accommodation for two weeks at a five star hotel).

Now he was on the way out, however, our five MPs had a problem. There were five candidates to succeed their inglorious leader. For a new MP, it was important to pick the winner and make sure everybody knew you were on the winner's side. Especially the winner.

If you chose a loser, everyone would always associate you with the loser. Your hopes of promotion and your chances of becoming Prime Minister one day would suffer a blow before your career even started. It was vital to choose the winner.

Our five politicians were among the 650 people returned from all over the country by the voters. They were all members of the same political party. It was called The Party. The main opposition was called The Other Party while there was also a small group of politicians who made up The Third Party.

Quite often The Party won elections. On this occasion, though, The Other Party won. Despite this, the five politicians managed to take their seats though The Party lost 62 constituencies altogether.

One of the famous five was just 23 years old when she became the Member of Parliament for Norfolk Seaside. Another was 32 when he was elected by the voters of Oxfordshire Camden. Two of them were 4, one was MP for Birmingham Quinton and the other was for Surrey eatherhead. The fifth was quite old. He was 44 when he became MP for the former coal-mining town of Blaydon near Newcastle on Tyne.

Why should we care about these five MPs? Everybody says politicians are all the same, out for what they can get. What's so special about these five compared with any other handful of grasping, untrustworthy know-nothings planning to lay down the law and tell us how to run our lives?

The answer is that one of these five will become Prime Minister in about ten years' time and the others will all pretend to be delighted. The other four will know with absolute certainty the one who becomes PM will be an utter disaster and they could do a much better job.

The first of the five, if only because she is the youngest, was the MP for Norfolk Seaside, Janet Roofer.

Janet's father was a shopkeeper and Methodist lay preacher. She adored him and rather disliked her frumpy mother as well as her younger sister who was not as clever and much less good-looking. Janet was clever and attractive.

She was educated at one of the country's last grammar schools where she did well enough to win a place at Cambridge University. She studied chemistry with a view to working on solutions to protect the country from climate change. For three years, she spent most of her time as the chair person of the university branch of The Party which was seen by everybody as a springboard to a political career.

Janet also had the wisdom and good sense to marry an older man, Jeff.

Jeff Roofer was a millionaire who was keen to see her succeed in politics. This was partly because he wanted to see his young wife fulfil her ambitions but also because having a wife as a Member of Parliament would be useful to his business. He was in oil, which was not a popular commodity because of climate change. It was important to protect the production and sale of oil as much as possible, for as long as possible. A wife in Parliament would be helpful in persuading politicians of the madness of their "green" policies.

Janet had never been to North Norfolk before she was selected as The Party's candidate for the constituency. Like every other constituency, it had about 70,000 adults eligible to vote – the smallest constituency had only 40,000 and the largest had 113,000 but in theory all MPs represented the same number of people so that everybody's vote was equal.

Janet's constituency covered a large area because it didn't include any big towns like Norwich or Cambridge. The roads were narrow so it took hours to drive from one side of the constituency to the other. Luckily Janet's husband provided her with a chauffeur so she could catch up with her Twitter feed between meetings.

The MP for Oxfordshire Camden was called Rick Clogg. Rick was married to a Brazilian model whose photograph adorned thousands of poster sites on the side of motorways and at roundabouts across the country promoting a brand of perfume. She was called Aurelia Sanchez and, for obvious reasons, continued to be called Sanchez after marrying Mr Clogg. She was about 12 inches taller than her husband, which made Rick look particularly insignificant when they were photographed together as a couple. Nobody understood what she could see in her millionaire husband.

Rick was educated at Eton and Oxford. He made a fortune in the City of London by spectacularly successful betting. He called it trading or investing or venture capital. In reality, it was betting that the value of a company would change significantly. Sometimes the value, based on the price of its shares, went up; sometimes the value fell. For a gambler – sorry, an investor – it didn't matter if the price went up or down as long as he speculated correctly.

Rick would sell shares he did not own for £5 each and, when the price fell, buy them for £2, making £3 per share profit on the deal. Or he would buy at £5 and sell at £8 if he thought the price would go up, making a profit of £3 per share yet again. As long as you guessed the right way, you could make lots of money. And Rick wasn't just buying and selling a single share; he was buying and selling millions of shares. So every deal made him more millions in profits.

Amateurs always lost money gambling like this on the stock market. Chaps like Rick Clogg made loads of it. They were professionals and they were helped by their friends. Most of their friends had also been to Eton and Oxford and several were in the House of Commons though most were in the House of Lords. They knew what's what and looked after each other with tips, in the same way racing fans pass on confidential information about horses.

Rick decided to go into politics because what was the point in having pots of money if you weren't famous? He was never going to make it as a film star or a pop singer so he had to think of something else. And as politics is show-business for ugly people, he decided to give it a go.

It wasn't difficult getting selected for the constituency of Oxfordshire Camden. He owned a small stately home in the area; just a few hundred acres managed by a clever chap called Caleb. Rick went hunting and shooting with all the important people locally. They were all influential members of The Party so they wanted one of their own to represent them in the House of Commons.

A constituency like Oxfordshire Camden is much sought-after by budding MPs. It is what's known as a "safe seat" because it more or less guaranteed The Party candidate a seat in Parliament.

Voters in Oxfordshire Camden have supported The Party's candidate at every election since women first got the vote in 1918. They disapproved of change back then and they disapprove of change now. So they elect the candidate for The Party. The Other Party and The Third Party always get a reasonable number of votes but the truth is, in Oxfordshire Camden, anyone wearing a rosette for The Party – a strange mauve colour – would win an election there even in a year when The Other Party was cleaning up elsewhere. They would elect a moderately intelligent pig in Oxfordshire Camden as long as it wore a mauve rosette and promised nothing would ever change.

Rick faced stiff competition to be chosen as the candidate for the constituency. Luckily for him, only 27 members of The Party turned up to decide who should represent them in Parliament and Rick knew all but three of them. He'd entertained them at home, taken them to open-air opera concerts or gone shooting with them. He was a close friend of the Master of Foxhounds who had brought along his wife, son, daughter and butler, all members of The Party, to vote for Rick.

The three Rick did not know were locals dragged there by one of the other candidates in the hope that, as his friends, they would vote for him. They probably did.

Rick had to give a speech which, according to everyone who heard it, was terrible. Rick said, 'I believe our children are our future.' One of his critics pointed out it would be very strange indeed if children were not the future.

Even so, Rick's chums secured him the vote. He was selected as The Party candidate for Oxfordshire Camden six months before the General Election. He resigned from his business and told his wife she would have to stop modelling now he was going into politics.

She agreed to spend two days a week in Oxfordshire campaigning for her husband. It worked brilliantly. Few people could resist the chance to have a selfie with a genuine supermodel. For a short time, Aurelia enjoyed herself. But she was more than happy to escape back to her London house at the first opportunity.

During the campaign, Rick visited some of the poorer parts of his constituency. The back streets where people smoked cigarettes, drank beer from cans and bought drugs. He was surprised to discover such places existed in this delightful part of beautiful Oxfordshire and swore never to visit them again. The people who lived there would never vote for The Party. They probably didn't vote at all, they were mostly out of heir heads. They were best avoided.

Rick was elected with a majority of 23,761. It was a few thousand own on the previous MP's majority. It was more than enough. Afterwards he joked, 'I'd happily lend some of my votes to other constituencies if it got a few of my colleagues elected. I've got so many votes I don't now what to do with them all.'

Most of his colleagues were envious of such a big majority and resented ick's boastfulness. Surplus votes in one constituency could not be transerred to another seat. Occasionally, the party winning the most seats at General Election and forming the new Government could take power espite having fewer votes than their opponents.

Many people thought this made the electoral system unfair but it as unlikely to change. After all, the winner who had taken power with wer votes than their opponents would never use that power to destroy eir own chances of winning power again next time.

One of those envious of Rick's huge majority was Parminder Grover, Sikh woman who won Birmingham Quinton with a majority of only ,236. It was called a "marginal constituency" because a few hundred otes either way could decide which candidate and which party won the lection there. Quinton sometimes elected The Other Party; sometimes elected The Party. Nobody could be sure who would win. Every vote ounted and all the parties spent time and as much money as they legally ould trying to persuade their supporters to vote.

It was illegal for a political party to spend more than a set amount in any one constituency during a General Election campaign. That sum is about £10,000 but it varies according to the number of voters in each constituency. All political parties bend these rules. They all cheat and spend more than they are allowed to on their "target" seats, that is, the marginal ones they must win if they're to gain a majority in Parliament and form a Government.

Very occasionally someone gets caught fiddling their election expenses and is sent to prison. Then everyone throws their hands up in horror says how terrible it is to cheat in this way and swears they would never be so under-hand.

They all lie.

Anyway, in the marginal seat of Birmingham Quinton, The Party selected an accountant as their candidate. It made sense. If anyone could cook the books and get away with it, then surely it had to be an accountant.

Parminder was a married mother of two young children who joined The Party when she was still a trainee accountant and spent the last three elections trudging round the streets of Birmingham sticking leaflets through letterboxes supporting other candidates who were all destined to lose. Birmingham, with 11 separate constituencies, mainly voted for The Other Party. Parminder was selected for Birmingham Quinton mainly because there was not much competition. Other members of The Party, especially those young university men planning a career making money followed by a career in politics – men like Rick Clogg, in fact – were not interested in a seat they probably would not win. Parminder thought it was her democratic duty to fly The Party flag even in some where as hopeless as Birmingham Quinton.

Yet improbably Parminder did win. The Other Party candidate was not very clever while Parminder was very bright. She was supported by her husband, Lennie, who had a business in the city selling shirts imported from India. She pushed her baby round in a pram with her little son toddling along at her side.

She said people were sick of The Other Party and the way it had been running Birmingham City Council so a vote for her would be a vote in protest at the local authority. They were especially upset about the city's 20 miles an hour speed limit and plans to build a massive new housing estate on the council-owned golf course.

Parminder successfully exploited their dislike of the council. It worked brilliantly even though Parminder's election would have absolutely no impact on speed limits or planning policy, because both of these things were decided by the local council. That's one of the beauties of elections – they are about whatever the voters want them to be about.

Horace Thompson, the new MP for Surrey Leatherhead, was two years older than Rick and Parminder. Like Rick, Horace didn't really have to count the votes cast for him at the election, he could just as easily have weighed them because he won by such a heavy majority. It wasn't quite as big as Rick's but 18,765 was not to be sneezed at. Horace's main opponent was not a member of The Other Party but a candidate put up by The Third Party, which was working hard in the leafy commuter belt around London to win support by opposing new housing development

– a policy The Third Party firmly supported elsewhere.

Horace was not married at the time of his election. His first wife and their three children lived in Wales. Horace visited them at Christmas. He was busy. He wrote for a newspaper (these were the days when people still did that and – even better –got paid well for doing so). He didn't give up his journalism when he became an MP partly because he liked the money and partly because it was so good for his public profile.

He had also written three books: A history of the Trojan wars, a biography of Alexander the Great and, when he was still at school, something about Byzantium which nobody had read and was out of print.

Like Rick, he had been to Eton and Oxford. Unlike Rick, Horace had not got a first-class degree but a 2-2. Horace said, 'If you get a First, you're a friend of the professor; if you get a Third, you're a friend of the professor. Only second-class degrees are truly first class.'

Rick never forgave him for that.

At the age of 44, Eric Orwell was quite old to be entering Parliament as an MP for the very first time. Eric had been leader of a local council somewhere grim in the North of England. He represented a former mining town called Blaydon, where they used to hold horse races. The town's big industry these days was data farming, with large warehouses stuffed full of computers whirring away all day long receiving and processing information about people's on-line activities.

The data was used by the Government, the police, MI5, MI6, GCHQ, big business, charities, local councils, energy suppliers, car manufacturers, shops and on-line fraudsters to track everyone's activities and swoop when needed.

Eric, who was married with two young children, was very proud that he had helped to attract the data farming company Obloquy to Blaydon. It's what secured him the nomination as The Party candidate at the election and won him election in a constituency which hadn't voted for The Party since 1923. Eric secured a majority of 4,321. It meant his seat was not secure but it was safer than Parminder's but nowhere near as safe as Rick, Horace or Janet's.

Eric was disadvantaged in other ways compared with his new colleagues. He had been a school-teacher so he wasn't rich. He employed his wife Sue as his secretary because the family needed the money now he had to commute 300 miles every week. The £81,000 a year he would now be earning was better than the combined income he'd been getting as a teacher and council leader but only just. And what with having to rent a flat in London and the crackdown on MPs' expenses, his finances were still tight.

Worse still, Eric had a Geordie accent. Some people thought this was charming. It was distinctive and recognisable, which helped him get better known. But it suggested he was a bit thick and should be walking the streets of Newcastle drinking brown ale and wearing a thin T-shirt even with snow on the ground.

STEP 2

Get to know your workplace

Eric, Parminder, Rick, Horace and Janet were on a tour of their new workplace.

The Houses of Parliament look like they were built in the Middle Ages but were actually put up in the mid-1800s after the old ones burnt down. There are two debating chambers. One, with green leather benches, is the House of Commons, which is for the 650 elected MPs. The benches are arrayed opposite each other. The front benches on each side are 13 feet apart which represents the length of two swords – to stop one MP drawing his sword on an opponent. Not that an MP would be allowed into the Commons debating chamber carrying a sword but even so, you can't take any chances when the arguments get heated.

From the chamber of the House of Commons, our MPs walked into the large central hall with its big mosaics of Saints George, Andrew, David and Patrick. They went down a plush corridor and through some impressive doors into the much smarter House of Lords with its red leather seats and the Throne where the Monarch sometimes sits.

These are the bits you see on TV. Our MPs felt impressed and a bit iggly. They felt like tourists or children on a school trip. This really idn't feel like a place of work.

The Lords are not elected. They are given their jobs. A few still have seat in the Lords because they inherited an aristocratic title. There are ome bishops from the Church of England with seats in the Lords. There re very many ex-MPs who get "shoved upstairs" as compensation for ailing to make a success of their political careers. One or two Peers et there because they have been big in business or sport or working for harities, or they were top civil servants. There are many Law Lords and ther legal eagles. Some people get to be members of the Lords not long fter they have donated millions of pounds to one of the political parties. The donations and the Peerages are not connected in any way, of course. Or, at least, that's what everybody says because selling seats in the House f Lords is illegal.

The House of Lords still has some power. It can temporarily reject r delay laws passed by the House of Commons. It can also check out ne detail of planned new laws and identify the flaws which need to be orted out before any harm is done.

Only Communist China has more people in a Parliamentary cham-er than the Lords, which has 788 members and isn't nearly big enough o accommodate them all. One day, three of our five MPs will end up on ne red benches, clad in crimson cloaks and ermine grinning foolishly at neir relatives in the public gallery.

The MPs' tour then led down long corridors, up stairs and along tore corridors. It took them into tiny little offices, small meeting rooms, rger committee rooms or even bigger restaurants. There were bars and shops. A post office. Offices for the hundreds of staff and police who worked there. There was a chapel in the basement and a rifle range which some MPs think should be turned into a swimming pool or a children's creche.

The MPs were then shown the Members' cloakroom where each constituency has its own peg and each peg has its own red ribbon. The ribbons are so MPs can hang up their swords before going into the debating chamber.

Finally, they were given the bad news about their offices. There were several within the big old building which is sometimes called the Houses of Parliament and sometimes the Palace of Westminster. Some of these offices were huge, with attractive views over Waterloo Bridge and the River Thames. The Leader of the Opposition had a suite of rooms. The Prime Minister had an office there as well as a home at Number 10, Downing Street. All the senior people had decent accommodation. Lower down the food chain, the offices got worse and worse. Some MPs shared cubby holes with one or two others plus their secretaries. These rooms were cramped yet they were almost all taken. Across the road, a five minute walk away down a secret tunnel under the road and past Embankment underground station, MPs could get to an ugly accommodation block called Portcullis House. It's named after the Parliamentary symbol of a portcullis. That symbol was designed by Sir Charles Barry when he built the Houses of Parliament in the 19th century. In 2018 MPs spent £50,000 redesigning the symbol. Nobody could tell the difference between the old symbol and the new one.

The offices at Portcullis House were more modern, bigger and more convenient but they were just that bit too far from where the action – and the gossip – was really taking place. Nobody wanted to be relegated to Portcullis House but that's where the five ended up.

The five were also taken through Westminster Hall, the only part of the old building to survive the fire in 1834. The Hall was built by King William II in 1097 and has seen it all – including the trial of King Charles I which led to his execution in 1649. In fact, within ten years, the House of Commons had asserted its importance to the nation by executing not just the King, but his chief adviser the Earl of Strafford, and the Archbishop of Canterbury.

'I can think of a few heads I wouldn't mind chopping off,' said Rick Clogg as their guide was pointing out the exact sport where Charles I sat during his trial.

'I've got a little list,' whispered Horace.

Janet Roofer frowned. Eric looked at Parminder. Parminder raised an eyebrow.

The Party eventually elected Samantha Toogood as their leader.

Samantha had once been Secretary of State for Health. She was good on the TV. People liked her. She had a sense of humour; she was quite stylish. She had a grown-up son and she was divorced, but on good terms, with her journalist husband.

Janet and Parminder were both vocal supporters, which was good for their careers. Horace and Rick were both vocal opponents. Eric tried to avoid making any public comment on the leadership election though, in the end, he came out in support of Sam Toogood when he was cornered by members of his constituency party and more or less forced to make a decision.

Samantha Toogood and her closest colleagues didn't pay much attention to what new MPs thought but they couldn't afford to ignore them either. Janet was earmarked for early promotion, mainly because she was so young. Parminder was less likely to make much progress because her constituency was so marginal she probably wouldn't survive the next General Election.

Rick was noted as a force to be reckoned with while Horace was unpredictable but looked good on the TV as well as having a sense of humour. People warmed to Horace and, though he opposed Sam as the new leader, the Prime Minister thought it would do no harm to make him part of her team to stop him trying to rock the boat.

'I'd rather have him inside the boat pissing out than outside pissing in,' said Samantha rather indelicately to the Chief Whip.

The Chief Whip was the MP in charge of making sure The Party's MPs voted the way the leader expected them to. His job was to stop rebellions. To bribe, cajole or threaten MPs who were threatening to vote the wrong way. He was also responsible for making sure these MPs kept on the straight and narrow – he wanted no scandals and, when they occurred, his job was to hush them up if he possibly could. The Chief Whip and his assistants, also called whips, are given their name after the whippers-in who stop hounds wandering away from the pack during a fox hunt.

Samantha and the Chief Whip didn't mention Eric Orwell at all. He was fat. He was old for a new MP. He spoke funny and he was from the

North. He was what's known as "lobby fodder" – someone who votes as he is told to vote, when he is told to vote, and expected to keep his head down and his nose clean at all other times. People like Eric Orwell were of little interest to their leaders or to anybody else for that matter.

Pretty soon the five MPs had to make their first speeches in Parliament. These used to be called "maiden speeches" but that was deemed sexist. Even so, it was still something of an ordeal which required lots of preparation, self-confidence, a decent joke if at all possible, and preferably nothing controversial because if you were to say the wrong thing it would not be forgotten. You might be stuck with it for ever.

Some MPs wait months before they make their maiden speech, others want to get it over with as soon as possible. One or two hope for a special moment, the moment when everyone will notice and they will be applauded as a rising star. A few use their maiden speech to raise a subject close to their hearts and rant about it gracelessly. Usually, these people are members of The Other Party.

Janet Roofer went early, keen to get it out of the way. She did as she was advised. She talked about how marvellous her predecessor as MP for Norfolk North had been. She spoke at length about her marvellous father and mentioned her mother too. She talked about her education, her training in chemistry, her husband. Most of all she talked about Admiral Lord Nelson, who won the Battle of Trafalgar in 1805 and died on his ship HMS Victory. That's because Nelson was born in her constituency. She concluded by saying, 'England expects every man – or woman – to do his – or her – duty.'

There were murmurings of support from those MPs in the House. Of the 650 who might have been there, perhaps 32 we actually in the debating chamber to hear Janet do her bit.

Next up was Rick Clogg, who talked a bit about the countryside in Camden. He didn't mention his predecessor or his wife or his family let alone his parents. He talked a lot about the economy and how it would be destroyed by the high tax plans of The Other Party and why the people of Britain would bitterly regret putting The Other Party in charge because they would only pick people's pockets.

Rick added that he was particularly concerned for young people and their education. 'I may have been to Eton,' he said, 'But we need good schools for all our children because our children are our future'.

Parminder was the most nervous of the first-timers. She had rarely made a speech in public and never in such a famous debating chamber. When she stood up to speak, at 6pm on a Wednesday evening, she felt sure there would be hardly anyone in the House to hear her. In fact, the Government had called a vote for 7pm requiring the presence of every MP. There was still an hour to go but some people thought it was too late for another cup of tea and too early for a drink so they drifted into the chamber only to discover newbie Parminder Grover on her feet delivering a speech written out on several sheets of A4 paper which were shaking about in her nervous hands.

Parminder talked about Birmingham, which was once the 'city of a thousand trades' but was now being ruined by The Other Party's policies. She spoke of speed limits and building on golf courses. She con-

essed she had a handicap of seven but feared now she was an MP she
couldn't have time to improve her golf. This was supposed to be a joke.
Unfortunately nobody laughed, which was a bit embarrassing and made
Harminder even more flustered. Still, she soldiered on and reached the
end without mishap. Several people congratulated her so it can't have
been all bad.

Nervousness was never Horace Thompson's problem. He barrelled
into the Commons chamber as if he owned the place. He tried to speak
like Winston Churchill.

In short bursts.

With long pauses.

And a gruff voice.

He quoted Aristotle and Thucydides. He made fun of The Other
Party. 'I was going to tell a political joke,' he said. Then paused. Looked
at the MPs on the opposite side and waved an arm in their direction as
he went on, 'I was going to tell a political joke but I see there is no need.
They have all been elected and are serving in the Government even as we
speak.'

Horace concluded by quoting his hero, Churchill, 'Courage is what
it takes to stand up and speak. Courage is also what it takes to sit down
and listen."

Horace did not make any friends among his political opponents. In
his own party some thought he was charming and charismatic, others
dismissed him as over-confident and brash. It would be discovered over
the coming years that, if it requires courage to sit down and listen to
other people, then Horace Thompson was a coward.

The last to make his first speech was the old man of the group, Eric Orwell. He'd been elected in May but it wasn't until November that he decided the time had come to break his duck. His speech was conventionally dull, praising his constituency, its history and people; thanking his family; congratulating his new leader Samantha Toogood on a speech she'd made a couple of weeks earlier at The Party's annual conference. He also talked about how The Other Party had neglected his constituency for years.

It was, according to the 25 MPs who listened to it and the two journalists who bothered to report on it, a safe, solid, rather dull speech. But workmanlike. Competent. Good enough for the pit, as people in Blaydon might say.

Why did you go into politics?

Over the next ten years, all five of our friends would be asked this question regularly. Sometimes they would be asked by a child during visit to a school in their constituency. On those occasions, their answer would vary a little but it would be based on, 'Oh I wanted to put something back' or 'Oh I wanted to change the world' or 'Oh our children are our future and I believe in our future and our children.'

Sometimes it would be asked by a stupid journalist. To a politician all journalists are stupid though some are also useful. A successful politician keeps one or two reporters in his pocket or purse. These reporters are fed little bits of gossip from time to time. The reporter realises that if his friend, let's say the MP for Surrey Leatherhead (Horace Thomp son) or the MP for Oxfordshire Camden (Rick Clogg), rises to the top of his profession, the reporter will rise as well. The value of his scoops will grow. He will become more important in his profession. He will be paid more.

Rick had a couple of "tame" journalists. But he knew he could never assume a reporter was really his friend. The moment the journalist discovers an MP has a secret mistress or a dodgy bank account in the Bahamas, he will reveal it to the world without a second's thought.

Still, when a reporter asks why you became a politician, it's as well to give an answer. Preferably one which won't come back to bite you. Do not say, for example, that you thought the existing crop were all corrupt and useless and you thought you could do so much better. Do say, you admire your colleagues and hope to learn from them. Do say, you wish to make a contribution, however small, to the well-being and development of your country. Do have one or two policies which you are known for. It could be education like Rick Clogg, or housing and speed limits like Parminder Grover. It could be a scientific response to the challenges of climate change, which was Janet Roofer's specialist subject. It might even be local government reform, the only thing Eric Orwell was known for. He had strong opinions and good ideas about a wide range of other subjects including health and education but nobody ever asked him because he once told a reporter he went into politics to reform local government.

Horace Thompson, on the other hand, had views on everything, all the time, and because he was amusing he got asked onto TV regularly. Some people thought he was a bit of a buffoon and, when he was asked why he went into politics, he would always answer, 'Because there is no position of World King, which is what I really want to be.'

People would laugh. Horace was never quite sure why because, for once, he wasn't joking.

STEP 3

Get re-elected and start climbing the greasy pole

After they had been in Parliament for four years, the five MPs faced a General Election. They were all successfully returned by their constituencies, which was surprising to Parminder and gratifying to Eric. Horace, Rick and Janice were neither surprised nor gratified. They took it for granted they would win again so they were not required to do much work or strain themselves unduly during the four weeks of election campaigning.

Eric and Parminder, on the other hand, spent every hour of every day tramping windswept streets knocking on doors, handing out leaflets and being insulted by passing drunks as they tried to win over the voters for a second time. Eric and Parminder both campaigned on the basis that a vote for The Party was better for the country than another term in office for the Government run by The Other Party. During The Other Party's time in power, they had put up taxes, the economy had slumped, the health service was a disgrace, schools were not educating their children properly, crime rates had risen, there weren't enough policemen and England had been knocked out of the World Cup without even getting to the finals.

This was enough to convince not only the people of Birmingham Quinton and Blaydon, Northumberland, that The Party and its leader Samantha Toogood were a better bet. The country as a whole came to the same decision. The Party won the General Election with a majority of just three.

That made things very exciting. Every vote in the House of Commons was on a knife-edge. If The Party didn't make sure all its MPs voted the same way, then its new legislation would be defeated. And if that happened too often, then there would be a vote of "no confidence" in the Government as a whole, and if the Government lost that, it would be out on its ear. The Prime Minister would have to call another election or – and this was worse – the leader of The Other Party might be asked to try forming a Government with the support of The Third Party not to mention a rag-tag army of other MPs from various outlying parts like Northern Ireland, Scotland and Wales.

The fear of that was enough to make most of The Party's MPs behave well enough. And because Samantha Toogood had such a small majority she had to keep as many of her own MPs on side as possible. It was time to hand out a few jobs to those MPs who had served their time on the back-benches.

Any MP getting a Government job for the first time was finally starting to climb 'the greasy pole'. It was called 'the greasy pole' because it was slippery and almost impossible to make it to the very top. In country fairs, there was usually a valuable side of ham at the top which everybody was keen to grab for himself. But the pole was so smeared with rease and pig fat that only the most lucky and determined ever came lose. Still, a junior job somewhere in the Government was where you ad to start if you wanted to make the attempt.

Parminder was asked to become a parliamentary private secretary to he Chancellor of the Exchequer. This is an unpaid job but it requires ard work and dedication, especially if you are working for someone eally senior like she was. As an accountant, at least Parminder could nderstand the figures prepared by her civil servants, which is more han could be said for her boss, the Chancellor, who was supposedly in harge of the nation's finances.

Rick was given a very junior minister's job at the Ministry of Clinate Change, a topic he knew nothing about and cared about even less. anet was made a junior health minister and immediately issued an order o National Health Service workers that anyone who was clinically obese ad six months to lose weight or they'd be out of a job, no matter if they vere a cleaner or a consultant. This didn't go down well with the unions ut it gained Janet a lot of publicity.

Horace was given a job working for the Chancellor of the Duchy of ancaster. This was an out-dated title for the Minister for the Civil Service. Horace's job, like his boss's, was a non-job shuffling bits of paper nd civil servants. It was dull and won him no publicity. Worse, he had o spend hours and hours in a committee room at the House of Comnons trying to guide a new piece of legislation, the Civil Service (Pay, Conditions and Terms of Service Amendment) Bill through its committe stage. This was a tedious, time-wasting process which meant a group f MPs scrutinised, line-by-line, each and every one of its 567 clauses.

The Opposition would sometimes demand changes to the proposed law. There would be mini-debates about this change or that. There would be a vote. The Government would win because it had a majority of MPs on the committee. This happened again and again. The Opposition never won a vote and nothing changed.

It was all very dull. Even so Horace managed to make headlines for all the wrong reasons when he was caught by a sharp-eyed member of The Other Party playing Candy Crush Saga on his phone when he should have been listening to an endless speech about the importance of trans gender rights in the field of foreign affairs at the Foreign Office.

Predictably, Eric was not given a job dealing with local government. Instead, he was sent to the Department for Work and Pensions where his in-tray consisted of complaints from old people who had been ripped off by pension funds – the sort of pension funds which handed their money to people like Rick Clogg to invest wisely on behalf of elderly pensioners.

Eric was upset to discover that one particular group of old folk had lost all their money while the man who ran the investment scheme still had homes in the Bahamas, Sandbanks, London and Switzerland. Eric decided that, lowly and dull though his job was, he had better do something about it. He thought it was wrong that a famous businessman could get away with fleecing little old ladies of their life savings and sit back in the sunshine on the Caribbean island he had bought with their money.

This became a big story. There were articles in the papers. Websites chased each other to expose the corruption. TV documentaries about the businessman and his many dodgy deals were made. All of these referred to Eric Orwell, the lowly Minister who had, according to them, launched a crusade against corruption in the pensions industry and was being hailed as the old people's hero.

Horace, Rick, Parminder and Janet were all green with envy.

Eric Orwell's success in rooting out corruption and standing up for old people meant he was getting noticed. At long last, people were interested in what he had to say. His constituents thought of him as a hero for working people. It was a pity his wife Sue didn't see it like that but in politics nothing was easy. Divorce was a hazard of the job. Sue stayed working as Eric's secretary in his constituency and they talked to each other almost every day. But Sue was tired of playing second fiddle to Eric's political career and left him for her optician, Dominic, who lived in nearby Barnards Castle. She took their two children with her and demanded half Eric's salary as maintenance.

His public career was taking off; his private life had crash-landed.

Janet Roofer, young, good-looking and married to a millionaire, was hated by doctors and nurses across the country. Her campaign against obesity in the National Health Service led to strikes, sit-ins and protest marches.

Janet was not sorry. 'If they are so upset,' she said on television, and later Tweeted to her growing army of followers, 'Why don't they go on hunger strike?'

That just made the whole thing even more controversial. Janet's enemies started to dig into her background. They could find nothing in her past that was shameful or likely to get her into trouble. They then started digging into her husband's past.

Jeff Roofer was 15 years older than his wife. He had "a past". That means he'd had girlfriends and good times. Pictures were dug up of him with his arms around various exotic young women. But as all this was before he met Janet, none of it did her any harm. And Jeff seemed to enjoy a bit of the limelight.

Rick Clogg was not making a good impression for himself at the Ministry for Climate Change. He was supposed to be in charge of forcing every motorist to abandon their petrol and diesel cars and switch to electric vehicles. But the wind wasn't blowing so the wind farms weren't generating electricity and there wasn't enough power to charge up all the electric cars on the roads. People were furious. They couldn't drive anywhere. They said there was no point in electric cars, the whole idea was madness and who cared about climate change anyway? The man in charge of Rick's department, the Secretary of State, decided this was not his problem it was the Junior Minister Rick Clogg's responsibility. So for days on end, Mr Clogg was sent out into the TV and radio studios to be abused by presenters, motorists, haulage companies, green-peace campaigners, political opponents, even members of his own party. He said it was an unfortunate consequence of decisions about the generation of electricity taken by Ministers going back 20 years. What he wanted to say was simply, 'It's not my fault, don't blame me.' But as far as everybody with an electric car was concerned, it was his fault and they did blame him.

Unfair, yes; but that's politics.

Horace, meanwhile, was holding curry and chips nights for his chums at his London townhouse which, he often said, was a terraced working man's place just round the corner from the Salvation Army hostel. This was strictly true. The house had once been occupied by a working man. Back when it was built in 1785. These days it was worth millions and was big enough for several working men or one ambitious Minister's third wife and growing family.

Horace enjoyed his curry and chips nights; so did his guests. Most of them were politicians but he often invited pop stars, authors, generals, admirals, impresarios, ballet dancers, Russians and Americans to his soirees. It was always entertaining to attend one of Horace's 'evenings'. Sometimes the Prime Minister herself would turn up for half an hour or so.

Horace did very little work as a minister for the civil service. It bored him. So when he was not playing Candy Crush he was writing books. He wrote a biography of David Lloyd George, the Prime Minister for much of the First World War. Lloyd George was Welsh and known for the many love affairs he had.

Horace knew things could only get better.

STEP 4

Try not to put your foot in it

After a few years of footling about in the lower leagues of politics, Rick Clogg got a big promotion. He became Minister of Agriculture, Fisheries and Food. He was a Cabinet Minister at last, with a big office and a chauffeur-driven electric Jaguar which did 120 miles between charges, just enough to get him back to his Oxfordshire mansion before it needed to be re-charged.

Rick was aware of the irony having spent so long defending electric vehicles, Government climate-change policy and praying for the wind to blow enough to turn the sails to make the turbines generate electricity to get people back on the road again.

People criticised the appointment of a rich Oxfordshire businessman to the role of the man in charge of agriculture. Especially the farmers. Although no farmer had been happy since 1846, the year the Government scrapped the corn laws which protected their income from foreign competition.

Rick promised to protect the nation's rural businesses and way of life.

A year later, after a Cabinet Minister was caught kissing his special adviser in his office and the news was plastered all over the internet, a vacancy arose for a new Health Secretary. The first candidate for the job only lasted six weeks before she was found to have wanted to privatise the NHS and had to resign. In her place, the job was offered to Parminder Grover, who became the first Sikh woman to run the NHS. This cut no ice with the doctors' trade union, the British Medical Association, which immediately demanded she sack Janet Roofer and reject the campaign against obesity.

'What are we to do, Janet?' Parminder asked her Junior Minister during their first meeting after the appointment was made public.how

'It's beginning to work, Secretary of State,' said Janet cheerfully. 'Weight-loss programmes are having an effect. The average weight of our employees has fallen by almost two pounds. Some people have shed two and a half stone. It's healthier for everyone and sets a good example to the rest of the country.'

Parminder was not a thin woman. Indeed, she often thought she should eat less, get more exercise, lose some weight but somehow she never managed to. Janet's campaign made her uncomfortable.

Janet, on the other hand, knew she, not Parminder, should have been given the Cabinet job. She knew she was still very young to achieve Cabinet rank but slimming down the NHS workforce was just the hors d'oeuvre of her political career. She needed to get her teeth into something more substantial and Parminder was in her way.

'I think we'd better drop the obesity campaign,' said Parminder.

Two days later, a story appeared on various websites saying the new

Secretary of State for Health had axed the obesity campaign because she knew she was too fat and lazy to follow it herself.

Janet denied any involvement in the story and who could disbelieve such an innocent and outraged-looking young woman?

After his success as champion of old people, newly-divorced Eric Orwell was delighted to be given a job in the Government whip's office. It was a job which prevented him from speaking in public. His role was to keep in constant contact with about 50 fellow MPs and make sure they voted as they were told to vote, spoke when they were told to speak, and supported the Government at every opportunity.

In his new job, Eric got to know his colleagues pretty well. He knew who was having an affair, and who it was with. He knew who was short of money and why. He had a little list of drunks. He knew which MPs were having nervous breakdowns. Who had a child up in court accused of arson. Whose brother-in-law was friends with a dodgy Kazakhstan arms dealer. Who was still taking money from an offshore bank account that could be traced back to a Russian oligarch who owned an English Premiership football club. He even knew which MP's wife voted for The Other Party and was trying to persuade her husband to switch sides.

Eric was a big man. People described him as 'bulky'. Sometimes it was necessary to use his weight in the course of his job. Once or twice some weedy MP threatened to take a stand as a matter of principle and vote against one Government measure or another. Eric would take them aside, into one of the many nooks and crannies in the Palace of Westminster where private conversations could take place with little risk of interruption.

One such "chat" was with the MP for Somerset Frome, a weedy little nerd called Rodney Wimpstone. Rodney opposed a Government plan to keep murderers in prison for the rest of their lives rather than letting them out after 10 or 15 years. Rodney said it was inhumane to give criminals no hope for the future. Eric pointed out that their victims had been deprived of any hope at all. Rodney said, even so. Eric grabbed him by the scruff of the neck, hauled him up against a wall where he had to stand on tip-toe while Eric whispered menacingly to him, 'Now listen you little creep, either you vote for this measure along with everyone else or your pathetic little political career is over. Finito. Ended. Adios. Sayonara. Gone. Lost. Disappeared down the toilet of history. Get it?'

'You can't threaten me,' said Rodney defiantly.

'I'm not threatening you, I'm telling you. There's a difference. What I am saying is you're doomed. It's not a threat, it's a promise.'

Rodney Wimpstone voted with his party after all, not against it. But he hated Eric Orwell ever after.

Horace Thompson swaggered into the Foreign Office as if he owned the place, though actually he was only a junior minister in the department responsible for nothing more exciting than Britain's relations with South America. At least it meant getting away from the lazy layabouts in the civil service. It meant foreign travel, which was fine by Horace. It meant chatting up Brazilian beauties. It even allowed him to enjoy intimate conversations with Rick Clogg's beautiful wife Aurelia Sanchez.

When Horace landed in Peru, on a mission to discuss the destruction of the Amazon rain forest, he said how great it was to be in Chile again, which was a bit embarrassing. Not as embarrassing as when he went to Venezuela and congratulated them for winning the World Cup, which was actually won by Brazil (again). Then he went to the Falkland Islands and suggested there might be a case for handing them over to Argentina after all. That caused outrage back home though he was hailed as a hero in Buenos Aires. It took Horace some time to explain that what he had actually said, or meant to say, or been misquoted as having said or otherwise having mis-spoken in some way, was that the Falklands were British and would always remain British as God intended.

He was recalled to London early from his tour of South America and, when he gave a press conference, he was told his tour had been a disaster.

Some politicians would have been aggressive in response to that. A few – the real failures – would have said how sorry they were for their utter incompetence. Horace just laughed and joked, 'There are no disasters, only opportunities. And, indeed, opportunities for fresh disasters.'

For some reason, everyone forgave him his laziness and incompetence and joined in the joke.

Horace was sent to negotiate a trade deal with the French-speaking West African country of Benin, where Voodoo is still a religion. It turned out one of Horace's great-grandmothers had been born there, that he spoke fluent French and they didn't mind when Horace started saying, 'I do do that hoodoo of the voodoo you do do here' to the locals when he went on walkabout.

Horace was a great success and came home with a trade deal and an agreement to protect the country's endangered lions.

Get re-elected again, promoted to the cabinet
(and try not to put your foot in it)

The law says Britain must have a General Election every five years. But they can be called earlier than that or, if a Government loses a vote of no confidence, they can be forced on a reluctant Prime Minister. Most Governments prefer to call an election after about four years rather than going the full five. That's because they have an element of surprise and they can call the election at a time when they think it will work best for their own party. That's the theory. But there is always speculation, rumour and gossip for months before an election is actually called so, when it is, nobody is very surprised.

What's more, Prime Ministers who 'go to the country' – an old-fashioned expression for calling a General Election – early sometimes discover things are not quite as easy as they expected. Theresa May called an election in 2017, three years early, expecting to increase her majority. All the opinion polls said she would win easily. In the end, she lost badly. It was a disaster and, although she struggled on as Prime Minister for another two years, nothing good came of it.

When Samantha Toogood called a General Election after four years in

ower, she was as sure as anyone can be of victory. The Other Party was
d by a very old ex-Communist who needed a nap for two hours every
fternoon and wore an old duffle coat at even the most solemn pub-
c occasions like Trooping the Colour and Remembrance Sunday. He
ad an undistinguished political career. He was a friend of the radical
Communists in Bolivia. He was a vegan who wore sandals with no socks
: every opportunity. As for The Third Party, it was being led by an
x-nursery school teacher who addressed the voters in the same way she
lked to three-year-olds: 'Now, voters, what do we want from a Third
arty Government? Yes, that's it. More taxes. And what's our favourite
olour? Green. Of course it is. Green is good.'

Samantha Toogood's Government cut taxes just before the election
as called. It meant that about a week before polling day, when every-
ne went to vote, they would find the money in their pay packets had
ucreased by about £30 a month. Mrs Toogood denied claims this was
 bribe. 'It's giving back money that belongs to the people in the first
lace,' she said, 'And it is a reward for all the hard work the people of our
reat nation have put in to turn round the fortunes of our economy after
 was almost destroyed by The Other Party.'

The voters took the money and voted Mrs Toogood back into Num-
er 10, Downing Street, where she lived with her husband, Derek, who
as more interested in Premiership football than he was in politics but
upported his wife as much as being an Arsenal supporter allowed.

The new Government had to have a new Cabinet.

At last, after years of hard graft, all the famous five got seats at the top
ble.

Rick Clogg was promoted to become Secretary of State for Education, the job he claimed he had always wanted.

Janet Roofer became Secretary of State for Health, succeeding her ex-boss Parminder Grover, who was made Home Secretary. Eric Orwell enjoyed the biggest promotion, becoming Chancellor of the Exchequer. Horace Thompson clawed his way into the Cabinet as Rick Clogg's replacement as Minister of Agriculture.

Government Ministers are always very cautious people. They know that if they say the wrong thing, it could lead to a financial crisis or shortage of eggs or something much worse like the end of their careers. They employ a small army of advisers, press officers, secretaries and civil servants to make sure they don't put a foot wrong. Sometimes things go wrong all the same.

Once they are outside the protective cocoon of Westminster, they find themselves exposed to real people. And real people have a habit of making life difficult for them.

Janet Roofer had never been forgiven by some people for her campaign against obesity. It wasn't just fat people either. A campaign group accused her of unlawful discrimination against the overweight. It said everyone had the right to eat as much as they liked and, anyway, some people were just genetically programmed to be obese.

When Janet visited a hospital as part of her job as Health Secretary, this group organised a protest. A barrier of 35 very fat people stood across the entrance to the place and refused to move when Mrs Roofer a very slim nine and a half stone – asked them politely if they would be kind enough to let her through.

The TV cameras caught the incident, which was a bit difficult for Janet. But worse was to come. During an interview with the telly people, a wireless microphone was attached to her lapel. Someone forgot to give it back so, when Janet retreated to her chauffeur-driven Jaguar with one of her aides, the TV people could hear it when she sighed deeply and said, 'Oh God how I hate fat people. Did you see the one in purple? Gross, gross, gross.'

Only then did the aide notice the microphone but it was too late. Janet's complaint made the headline news all over the country – in fact, all over the world.

There were calls for her resignation. She had to explain herself to the Prime Minister, Mrs Toogood. She survived because it was deemed she was doing a good job and this was her first really big mistake. And many people agreed with her – even if they were too afraid to say so.

Eventually, Mrs Roofer was forced to seek out the woman in purple. She was a social worker whose hair was the same colour as the dungarees she was wearing on the day she blocked Janet's way into the hospital. They met in front of the TV cameras at a café where Janet was obliged not only to apologise profusely for the rude things she said about the woman in purple but, by way of making up for it all, she had to eat not one, not two, but three cream-and-jam filled doughnuts and agree they were very tasty indeed.

Parminder Grover made the mistake of criticising the police. It was not unusual for Home Secretaries to complain about one aspect or another of the way the police behaved. Parminder, taking a leaf out of Janet Roofer's book, said she thought all police officers ought to be able to run a mile without collapsing. How, she said, could an officer expect to catch a robber if he wasn't fit enough for a decent foot-race? Some Chief Constables decided to introduce compulsory fitness sessions for police officers on the beat. The officers asked why they should be expected to undergo fitness classes when their superiors were allowed to sit behind their desks. Eventually the idea was quietly dropped.

But when Parminder visited a police training college on one of her many publicity drives, she was challenged to a race by a couple of the officers. This was supposed to be a friendly gesture, as if the whole thing was being done for a laugh.

Parminder was approaching middle-age. She'd had two children. She was far too busy to take proper exercise. And yet, against the advice of her press officer, she accepted the challenge. Someone found her some running kit. She disappeared to change into it and emerged onto the running track alongside three women police officers who all looked frighteningly young, fit and determined.

There were forced smiles all round.

It was a 100 metres track. Parminder was given a 30 metre start on account of her age. When the gun went for the start of the race, Parminder summoned up all the strength she could manage, the determination, the gritted teeth and set off as fast as she could. After six or seven metres something happened. A terrible pain shot up her right leg. She yelled in agony. Three police women came flying past her. She hobbled on for a few paces and collapsed in agony. A torn muscle.

This all made an amusing snippet on the evening news. It took Parminder three months to get over the pain and throw away her crutch.

For Horace Thompson there was worse.

His job involved visiting agricultural shows up and down the country. These were often muddy affairs with cattle muck, tractors and horses cluttering up the place.

Horace was expected to smile and demonstrate his love of all animals. He was also expected to remain upright at all times. When he was bowled over by an angry sheep, it was amusing. Luckily the TV cameras missed it and the picture only appeared in the local paper.

At another show, he was dumped on a hay bale by an over-enthusiastic pony. This was OK though also a bit humiliating. The day some angry farmers poured liquid manure over the drive of his Surrey home was annoying but actually won him a little public sympathy.

Disaster struck when Horace went to the Wessex show to give out an award to the Farmer Most Outstanding In His Field. As Horace was striding purposefully forward to present the prize, he slipped on the wet grass and slid embarrassingly into a pool of mud and horse manure. He was covered in muck from head to toe. Unfortunately, a TV documentary team was following him at the time. The moment he slipped into the manure was broadcast not just in the programme itself but in every promotional advertisement for the show. The clip was so funny it became a big hit on Twitter and Instagram. "Horace's shit show" was the headline.

The interesting thing was that, no matter how bad the humiliation seemed, Horace always got up again, smiling and joking.

Rick Clogg was always visiting schools. As Education Secretary it was his job, though most teachers seemed to loathe him. He couldn't understand why. On one of these visits he attended a class of 12-year-olds who were undergoing a spelling test.

A child would be called to the front of the classroom, in front of the Minister, his staff, the TV cameras, their friends and their teacher, and asked to write the correct spelling of a word on the blackboard.

The first kid had to spell "neighbour", did so correctly and got a round of applause.

The second had to spell "thieves" and got her round of applause.

The third child, a boy called Charlie, was asked to spell "potato". He did as he was asked and won his applause.

The Education Secretary stopped him before he could return to his desk. 'Just a minute,' said Rick with a smile. 'Where's the e?'

The boy looked puzzled.

'Potato is spelt with an e,' said Rick, picking up a piece of chalk and adding the letter to the end of the word so it read 'potatoe'.

The teacher looked embarrassed. The Minister's aides looked embarrassed. Charlie looked puzzled. His classmates looked puzzled. The TV cameras kept whirring away.

The next day one of the papers showed Rick as a potato with the head-

ne "Mr Potato Head". Rick's spelling mistake lived with him for the
est of his career. Some people started to call him Rickey the Educatione
ecretaree. In the House of Commons, various Opposition MPs started
heir questions to him in mock Yorkshire accents, going, 'Eeee, will the
Minister confirm….' or 'Eeee, when will the Minister decide….' He was
ent potatoes through the post. He blamed the briefing notes he'd been
iven before visiting the school but that didn't slice no chips with the
otato-buying, spelling-loving, voting public.

Eric Orwell, Chancellor of the Exchequer, was not terribly popular.
He'd increased taxes and cut public spending. He said the country could
ot afford to carry on living as if there were no tomorrow – one day, its
ebts would have to be paid off and now was the time to get it under
ontrol again. This meant cutbacks. It meant bigger school classes. It
eant fewer ships for the Royal Navy and even no new hospitals. Every-
ne hated him – except the people who agreed the country was heavily
 debt and needed to do something about it.

It was going well enough for Eric until someone – his ex-wife, he
sumed – put a bank statement on line. It was taken down pretty quickly
ut not before the world discovered that the prudent, careful, cautious
hancellor of the Exchequer was tens of thousands of pounds in debt.

Why was he in debt? Where had the money gone? Was he incapable
f managing his own finances? If so, why should we trust him to man-
e the country's? The questions swirled around for days as the media
lunged into investigating as much as they could about Rick's personal

finances. His ex-wife was most helpful to them, complaining he still owed her money, that he was in arrears with the alimony he owed her and he hadn't seen his children for weeks. There were dark hints that Eric was spending the money on a young woman though if that was true there was no evidence to prove it and nobody came forward to claim they were his girlfriend.

Eric said it was a private matter and he was not willing to discuss his personal finances in public. The questions wouldn't go away. Eventually he was forced to make a statement in Parliament explaining the money was raised to buy a new house in his constituency and pay off his ex-wife. He admitted he was living beyond his means and made it clear he would be able to pay off all his debts once his political career came to an end and he was able to earn real money again. Many of his enemies said he should be able to make ends meet on a salary of £153,000 a year when the minimum wage was just £8.91 an hour.

Eventually one of The Party's millionaire supporters bailed him out though this was also made public and caused another scandal.

It was all very embarrassing.

STEP 6

Never answer the question

Every aspiring politician needs to learn one vital lesson: Never, ever, ever, ever answer the question. Always change the subject. Always stick to the thing you went on the TV or radio to talk about and ignore, as far as you possibly can, the impertinent questions stupid, untrustworthy, unreliable journalists will try to embarrass you with.

They want to make you look an idiot. You want to avoid looking an idiot.

'So Minister, how do you spell "cemetery"?'

'I'm not getting into this.'

'Minister, how do you spell "receive"?'

'I am here to talk about this year's A-level results and our excellent record at raising standards in the classroom.'

'But raising standards must include spelling, Minister. I'm sure you agree. And it must be important for the Secretary of State for Education to be able to spell. Isn't that right, Minister?'

'I know what you are trying to do and I will not allow it.'

'I'm sorry, Minister. Our viewers have a right to know whether the politician in charge of the nation's schools and universities is able to spell common words correctly.'

'We now have 53 per cent of school leavers going on to higher education. We have more young people in apprenticeship schemes than ever before. We are raising standards for 11-year-olds. We have more nursery places than ever before. We have more teachers than ever before. Our record speaks for itself.'

'But can all these young people spell potato, Minister?'

'This is ridiculous.'

'What are seven eights?'

'What?'

'Seven eights, Minister. Simple maths.'

'I'm not getting into this.'

'Times tables, Minister.'

'No. I'm not getting into this. No.'

'So Minister, is it true you hate fat people.'

'I have already apologised for this and apologised in person to the lady involved.'

'But you said you hated fat people.'

'I made a comment, which I should not have made, in the privacy of my own car...'

'A Ministerial car, Minister.'

'I don't see the difference.'

'A Ministerial car is not private, Minister. You have a civil servant as your chauffeur.'

'Our drivers have signed the Official Secrets Act.'

'Does that cover Ministers who hate fat people.'

'I have apologised for that. Now can we move on? I am here to talk about the £350 million we have invested in this magnificent new hospital. It is being staffed…'

'With fat people, Minister?'

'With the best nurses, doctors and ancillary staff we can recruit and we are recruiting more people than ever before thanks to the generous pay and conditions we have negotiated for our hospital staff. And I would like to take this opportunity to thank each and every one of our hospital staff for the marvellous life-saving job they do, day in and day out, 24 hours a day, 365 days of the year.'

'Even the fat ones, Minister?'

'So, Minister, I see you are still using a walking stick. Do you now regret saying police officers are unfit?'

'I regret challenging three fit young women to a race, certainly.'

'They were much fitter than you, weren't they?'

'They were. But the lesson was a good one. Many officers, like many politicians, lead sedentary lives. They do not get enough exercise. They could never catch up with a robber. They'd end up like me, pulling a muscle.'

'So you do regret saying officers are unfit.'

'It was a challenge, not a statement. It was a question. Are all our police officers as fit as they really should be? I am not sure of the answer.'

'Minister, is this incident the most embarrassing of your career?'

'What I am not embarrassed about is the way we have reduced the crime rate by seven per cent. I am not embarrassed that we have more officers on the beat. I am not embarrassed that we are cracking down on knife crime. I am not embarrassed that we have more women in the top jobs and more transgender officers than ever before.'

'But are they fit enough, Minister?'

'Chancellor, when you were a Government whip a few years ago it is alleged you grabbed one of your own MPs by the scruff of the neck, held him up against a wall and threatened to punch his face unless he voted the way you told him to?'

'Who said that?'

'It is in the memoirs of your former colleague Rodney Wimpstone.'

'Is it? Well well. You mean the MP who crossed the floor of the Commons to join The Other Party.'

'Because of your violence, he says, Minister.'

'I'm not sure the word of a politician who is elected by his constituents as an MP for The Party and then goes back on his word and joins The Other Party can be trusted with anything he says.'

'Are you saying he is lying, Minister?'

'I am saying you cannot trust what the man says.'

'So he is lying, is he, Minister?'

'His word cannot be relied upon.'

'Is he lying, Minister? Yes or no?'

'What I am saying is that an MP who betrays his constituents by switching from one political party to another...'

'Is he lying, Minister? Yes or no?'

'Look, this is a politician who was once a member of The Party...'

'Yes or no, Minister? Yes or no?'

'This has nothing to do with the state of the British economy. We have record levels of employment, low inflation, low interest rates, record levels of investment...'

'But Mr Wimpstone, Minister. Are you saying he is a liar? Yes or no?'

'We are seeing good, steady economic growth...'

'It's a simple question, Minister. Yes or no?'

'The Bank of England economic forecast suggests growth of at least one and a quarter percentage points over the next three quarters...'

'And that is all we have time for this evening. Thank you, Chancellor.'

'Horace Thompson. Minister. You have upset the French by threatening to restrict their fishing rights.'

'Oh donnez-moi un break. C'est impossible. Les Francais are notre amis. La belle France is one of my favourite countries. Last night I was in the bath singing "Je ne regrette rien".'

'Minister, are you saying you don't care whether you have upset the French or not?'

'Of course not. J'aime beaucoup les French. Unfortunately they do not like us because we are always having to come to their rescue. Did you know that during the French revolution, we took in hundreds of refugees? C'est terrible but ce n'est pas la gare.'

'La gare?'

'The station. Or should it be la guerre? French is only my fourth language.'

'Fishing rights, Minister?'

'D'accord. Nobody has more respect for the average French matelot than I do, nobody. I have gone fishing in France. You could say I am French fisherman. But they are our cod and to the British, cod is God.'

'So you won't be apologising to the French, Minister?'

'Apologise? Oui et non. Indeed. Oui et non.'

'Yes or no, Minister?'

'Indeed. Of course. D'accord. Ca ne fait rein. Or should I say, "Say fairy Ann"?'

STEP 7

Never let a good crisis go to waste

There was a political crisis.

There is always a political crisis.

When, many years ago, Prime Minister Harold MacMillan was asked what was it that shifted Governments off course, he replied, 'Events, dear boy. Events.' Nothing much has changed since then.

One day everything is trotting along smoothly enough. Then something happens. It can be something massive, like the day terrorists flew planes into the twin towers in New York; it can be something bizarre, like the day there was a run on an obscure building society in the North of England that almost destroyed the entire capitalist system; it can be something only too human, such as the time a Government Minister for War lied in the Commons about having an affair with a Russian spy; it can be something tragic, like the global coronavirus pandemic.

You don't know what the crisis will be until it happens but when it does it is a nightmare for politicians.

They are the ones people look to for leadership. But none of them signs up for crisis management. Most of them don't have a clue what to do when something terrible happens. They rely on advisers. Even the advisers often don't have a clue what to do. When a crisis really does happen, it's usually a case of the blind leading the blind. Political leaders have to give every impression they are in control and they know what they're doing.

The truth is they are not in control and they don't know what they're doing.

The crisis that swamped Samantha Toogood's Government came when the Chinese Government banned the export of toys to Britain.

It might not sound like such a big deal but it turned out almost all the toys bought in Britain were made in China. Model cars, trains, dolls, almost all the equipment needed for computer games, you name it, if it's a toy it's almost certainly made in China. Even Lego is made in China – a fact known by very few people until the Danish company announced there would be no more Lego sold in Britain because of the Chinese export ban.

How had this extraordinary ban come about? Samantha Toogood's Government protested at the way the Red Army of the Chinese Communist Party invaded Hong Kong, locked up hundreds of students and nationalised a British bank. Mrs Toogood asked the United Nations to intervene. The Chinese objected. Britain said China was a repressive police state. The Chinese said, in that case you won't want our toys any more will you and that was that.

No more toys.

This was in August, just as shops and websites were stocking up for Christmas. The papers announced that Christmas would be ruined for millions of children. "No Santa this year," they announced and "Christmas is cancelled".

Attempts were made to import toys from other countries like France, Germany and the United States but they said they only had enough for their own kids and couldn't spare any for Britain even if we paid twice the usual price for them.

Mrs Toogood's Ministers tried their friends in Australia and Canada, New Zealand and India but without much success though they did secure a supply of boomerangs and cuddly koalas.

Most people agreed with the Government when it condemned the destruction of freedom in Hong Kong. But they were not so happy with the Christmas toy shortage. Things deteriorated very quickly as children were interviewed on TV, told there would be no stocking from Father Christmas this year and burst into tears.

Eventually Mrs Toogood was forced into a humiliating climb-down. She apologised to China and sent her Foreign Secretary to Beijing to beg the Communists to start sending over their toys again. But it was all too late to save Christmas.

In early December, The Other Party tabled a vote of no confidence in the Government. Despite Mrs Toogood's majority of 38, she only survived by six votes. Several of her MPs abstained, staying away from the Commons altogether to avoid having to vote either for or against her;

three MPs actually voted with the Opposition against their own Prime Minister.

It was too bad for Mrs Toogood.

After the vote, late in the evening, she sat in her big office in the Houses of Parliament and drank whisky with the Chief Whip. They surveyed the voting figures mournfully. Then, one by one, Samantha called in each member of her Cabinet. She asked them the same question, 'Do I still have your support?'

They had all voted for her because you couldn't stay in the Cabinet and vote against your own Government. But that didn't mean they really supported their leader.

One after another the Ministers came into the office and pledged their support. Or at least suggested they might still support her if she promoted them or sacked someone else or changed this policy or that policy. Parminder Grover said, 'Of course you have my full support Prime Minister but while I'm here I wonder if I can ask about the money for extra police officers. I think £1 billion should do it.'

Rick Clogg said, 'Of course you have my full support, Prime Minister. But you must appreciate the weight of opinion is against you. I am sure you will survive this crisis Prime Minister and feel sure you will remember those of your colleagues who have remained most loyal to you.'

Horace Thompson said, 'Of course you have my full support, Prime Minister. But I would very much appreciate a return to the Foreign

Office. I think your Government needs a new Foreign Secretary.'

Eric Orwell said, 'No, Samantha, you must not resign. The people stabbing you in the back are traitors. You must stay and defy them. We need you, Sam. I need you.' Eric was close to tears when he left his friend the Prime Minster.

Last to see her was Janet Roofer. She was blunt. 'I am sorry, Samantha, but I cannot possibly support you in office any longer. The position is disastrous and will not improve unless you depart. In the words of Oliver Cromwell, "You have sat too long for any good you have been doing lately. In the name of God, go!"'

'Thank you for your honesty, Janet,' said the Prime Minister.

'It's not what you want to hear, I know that,' she said, 'But someone has to tell you the truth.'

The next day, a weeping Samantha Toogood announced she would be leaving Downing Street just as soon as her party had chosen her successor.

This is, of course, a personal tragedy for poor Mrs Toogood. All that power and fame suddenly drained away. For her, the long years ahead would be a boring, dull anti-climax and as she looked back on her career, she would always be disappointed and frustrated.

For everyone else, it was an exciting opportunity. The survivors of Mrs Toogood's disaster – when she fell some of her closest supporters fell with her – discovered a new lease of life.

The famous five, now among the most senior politicians in their party, had one idea in common.

Now was the time. Now was their time. It might never come again.

It was now or never.

This was their chance, probably their one and only chance. To make history. To become Prime Minister.

It was such a delirious idea none of them thought much beyond the day they could walk into Number 10 in front of the cameras, waving and smiling, to become the new Prime Minister of Great Britain and Northern Ireland. It was, in truth, the only real reason why they ever went into politics in the first place. Any MP who denies he or she would like to be Prime Minister is not telling the truth. Every MP wants to get the top job even though they know hardly anybody will succeed and even though the people who do get it invariably end up making a terrible mess of it. In politics, every career ends in failure yet no politician admits this sad fact because they know they will go down in history which, they think, makes the heartbreak when it ends worthwhile. When the job vacancy of Prime Minister arises, anyone with the slightest chance of getting the top job starts to weigh up their chances of success.

In The Party, the rules for selecting a leader kept changing whenever the winner turned out to be a failure. At the time of Mrs Toogood's resignation, it was decided the winner would be the one who got a majority of the votes of their fellow MPs. The Party would not consult its members; there wasn't enough time. The Government had to carry on in power. Just because the party changed its leader didn't mean the collapse of the Government nor did it require a General Election, though plenty of its opponents demanded one.

The question would be decided by the 344 members of The Party without reference to anybody else.

Horace Thompson was seen in the Commons tea room on the afternoon Mrs Toogood announced her resignation. He moved from one table to the next, chatting with his colleagues in The Party, slapping them on the back, laughing and joking, looking serious when required. He drank a great deal of tea and shook a great many hands. Then he went off to give six TV interviews.

'Horace is on manoeuvres,' one of his opponents said.

Parminder held a meeting with five of her closest Parliamentary friends, one of whom was in the House of Lords and wouldn't have a vote. The question was: should she run for the leadership? Did she stand a chance or would she be humiliated? They persuaded her to give it a go. She didn't need much persuading.

Janet Roofer was stuck in a cubby-hole office dealing with emails from her constituents when Sir Richard Hunter and Sir Adrian Hicks politely asked if they could come in. These two were elder statesmen of The Party. They'd been around for years. Both were well-connected.

'Mrs Roofer, Janet,' said Sir Adrian in his usual unctuous style, 'We are here representing a group of concerned members who believe the time has come for The Party to change course. A new look. A younger look. We need to expand our support beyond the old and middle-aged. We need someone attractive to young people. In short, Mrs Roofer, Janet, we need you.'

Chancellor of the Exchequer Eric Orwell had no choice but to stand for the leadership. He knew if he didn't get the top job, whoever took over as PM would sack him straight away. His austerity policies were unpopular. The new leader would need a Chancellor prepared to spend money whatever the long-term consequences. If he sat on his hands and let the leadership election take place without him, he was doomed anyway. Better to go down fighting. Eric Orwell was the first of the five MPs to get ten colleagues to sign a document nominating him as a candidate for the leadership. He was the first to announce this decision in public. And the first to make a speech in public.

Rick Clogg persuaded his beautiful wife to stand with him on the steps of their smart Georgian town house in London to announce his decision, reluctantly and with many reservations, to allow his name to be put forward as a candidate for the highest political office.

Rick said it was a matter of deep personal regret that the loyal, dedicated and patriotic Samantha Toogood had felt it necessary to tender her resignation and what the country needed now was strength and stability, vision and experience. Rick reminded his audience, 'Our children are our future.'

To become Prime Minister, you have to reveal a ruthlessness and cunning your best friends never thought you were capable of. It's not good enough simply turning on your Prime Minister when she needs you most, as Janet Roofer did when she told Samantha Toogood it was time for her to quit.

Janet Roofer spent several years as Mrs Toogood's best friend in politics but when the moment came for her to strike, friendship and loyalty meant nothing at all.

Eric Orwell, on the other hand, was upset by the way Mrs Toogood was treated. He was loyal to her but not so much to his own best friend in politics, the Defence Secretary Chris Miller. Eric and Chris were both MPs from the north of England, they shared a flat in London for many years and they often debated what The Party's policies should be. One of them had to fight for the leadership but when Chris Miller told Eric he was thinking of going for it, his best friend said, 'I wouldn't do that if I were you, Chris.'

'What do you mean?' asked the Defence Secretary.

'Well, at the moment I don't think anyone knows your sister-in-law is the owner of that company your department has just given a £2 billion contract to. You wouldn't want that to come out during the leadership election, would you?'

'Is that some sort of a threat, Eric?'

'Not a threat, old boy, just friendly advice.'

Rick Clogg stayed at home with toothache for a few days.

This was a tactical toothache.

He didn't want to be seen to be betraying Mrs Toogood but he didn't want to be seen to be supporting her either. The best policy was to lie low and do nothing. His tactic was to stay out of trouble while the dust settled then get in there and start knocking down his opponents.

Parminder Grover issued what she called "A Brummie Manifesto". It set out her "vision" for the country. It was actually written by a woman who had been employed as Parminder's political adviser for some time. Parminder claimed it was all her own work. When the adviser suggested she wrote it, Parminder very publicly declared, 'If I had to rely on her for political advice, I would still be wandering the streets of Quinton as an out-of-work city councillor. We parted company months ago because her advice was so unreliable.'

Horace Thompson had a long-standing deal with Mike Stove, the Trade Secretary, that when the top job became vacant, Horace would support Mike. They knew if Horace threw his weight behind Mike, then tove's campaign would be unstoppable.

A press conference was called. Stove planned to announce he was :anding for the leadership of The Party and therefore would become the ext Prime Minister.

Before his friend took to the stage, however, Horace announced, 'We eed someone who is be able to build a team, lead and unite. I hoped 1at person would be Michael Stove. But in the last few days I have come, :luctantly but firmly, to the conclusion that while Mike has great attri- utes, he is not capable of uniting that team and leading the party and 1e country in the way that I would have hoped. It has to fall to some- 1e else, someone who's experienced at the highest levels in the Cabinet. has to fall to me.'

The press conference was abandoned. Michael Stove had to give up n the idea of becoming Prime Minister. He and Horace never spoke to ich other again.

So there we are. Five candidates for the top job.
Rick Clogg, Parminder Grover, Janet Roofer, Horace Thompson and ric Orwell.
Which one should become Prime Minister?
The answer to that question, dear reader, is up to you. But see page one fore casting your vote.